To Hannah..

May you always be free..

Lais Sal
New York
2019

www.mascotbooks.com

The Silent Nightingale

For more information, please contact:
Mascot Books
620 Herndon Parkway, Suite 320
Herndon, VA 20170
info@mascotbooks.com

Library of Congress Control Number: 2017916324

CPSIA Code: PBANG0218A
ISBN-13: 978-1-68401-563-4

Printed in the United States

العندليب الصامت

THE SILENT NIGHTINGALE

تأليف لميس سليمان السليم   Written by Lamis S. Solaim

رسومات ايرين نوواك   Illustrated by Erin Nowak

إلى أبي،

لازلت أسمعك تغني

To my father,

I still hear you singing

هرع سليمان ونواف إلى داخل
المنزل بحماس "لقد أمسكنا بطيرا!"

Soliman and Nawaf ran into
the house with excitement.
"We caught a bird!"

إنه ليس أي طير...إنه عندليب..تأملوا جماله "قالت سارة ".

"That's not just any bird, it's a Nightingale!"
said Sara. "It's BEAUTIFUL."

"Let's build a cage, so it won't fly away," suggested Aziz.
"Yes, let's make it a castle! Fit for a GORGEOUS bird," said Basma.

"لابد أن نبني له قفصاً حتى لا يهرب" قال عزيز.

"نعم قفصٌ كالقصر يليق بهذا الطائر الجميل"
أجابت بسمة.

"لماذا لا يغرد؟" تساءلت العنود.

"Why doesn't it chirp?" Anoud wondered.

"ربما علينا أن نقوم بتزيين القفص كي يشعر بالحميمية" اقترحت العنود.

"Maybe we should decorate the cage so
it feels cozy," suggested Anoud.

هرعت ياسمين ولولو
لجلب الشرائط اللماعة وحبات اللؤلؤ والريش وبدأن بتزيين القفص.

Yasmeen and Lulu ran to fetch glittery ribbons, feathers,
and some pearls. The girls then started decorating the cage.

أصبح القفص خلاباً!......
ولكن العندليب ظل صامتاً.

The cage looked SPECTACULAR!
But still, the Nightingale remained silent.

دخل سلمنكي حاملاً صينية من الفاكهة الشهية..

"لا شيء يجلب السعادة مثل
وجبةٍ لذيذة، سيغرد بعد أن يشبع."

Salamanki walked in carrying an appetizing
fruit tray. "Nothing brings joy like a tasty meal!
It will start singing once it's full."

ولكن العندليب
ظل صامتاً.

But still,
the Nightingale
remained silent.

"قد يغني إذا استمع إلى الموسيقى"
بدأت هيا بعزف لحن هادئ على الكمان.

"It may start singing if we play some music," Haya
suggested, raising her violin to play a soft melody.

ولكن العندليب ظل صامتاً.

But still, the Nightingale
remained silent.

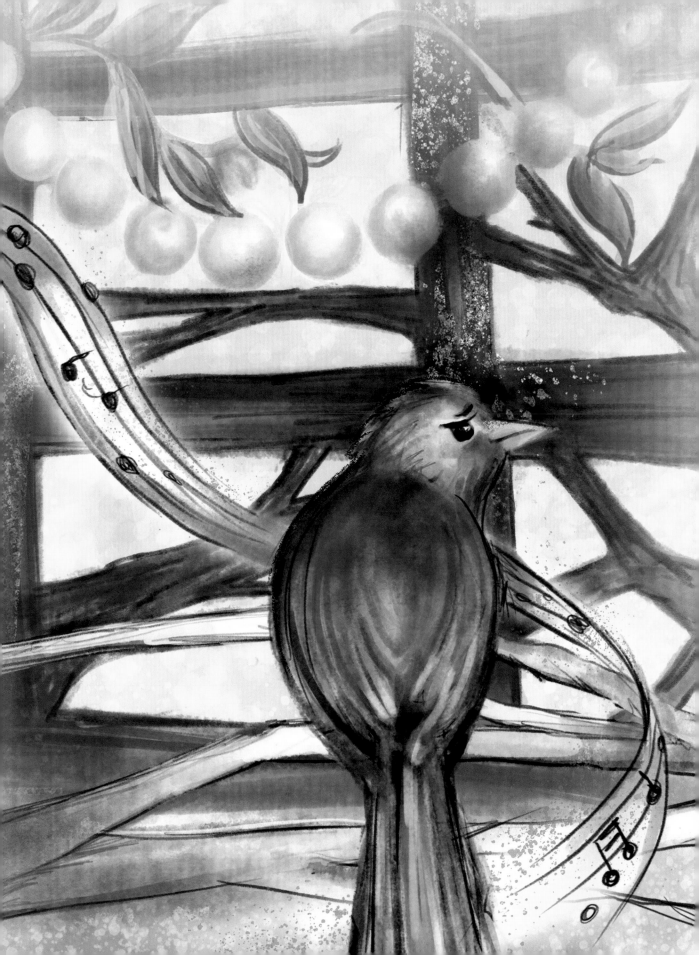

جرّب الأطفال حركاتهم البهلوانية، لعلّ الطّيْر يشعر بالسعادة ويغني.

The little ones tried their acrobatic moves to cheer the bird up, hoping it might start singing.

ولكن العندليب
ظل صامتاً.

But still, the
Nightingale
remained silent.

شعر الأطفال بالإحباط واليأس.

The children became
frustrated and gave up.

سمع الأطفال صوتاً هادئاً من الغرفة المجاورة.. إنه

بابا سليمان يغني لصغيرته نورة بصوته الحنون ..

سمعتُ شعراً للعندليبِ

A soft lullaby came from
the other room. It was
BaBa Soliman singing
to little Noura in his
soothing voice.

تلاه فوق الغصنِ الرطيبِ

ياقومُ إني خُلقتُ حرّاً

لم أرضى إلا الفضا مقرّا

"I once heard a nightingale singing,
Its words so full of meaning,
Once high on a tree,
He sang, 'I've always been free.

فإن أردتم أن تؤنسوني

ففي المباني لا تحبسوني

وإن اردتم أن تنطقوني

The WORLD is my home,
You see, I was born to roam,
So the only way I will be happy,
Is without others trying to trap me,

And for me to sing, my only plea,
Is for you to...'"

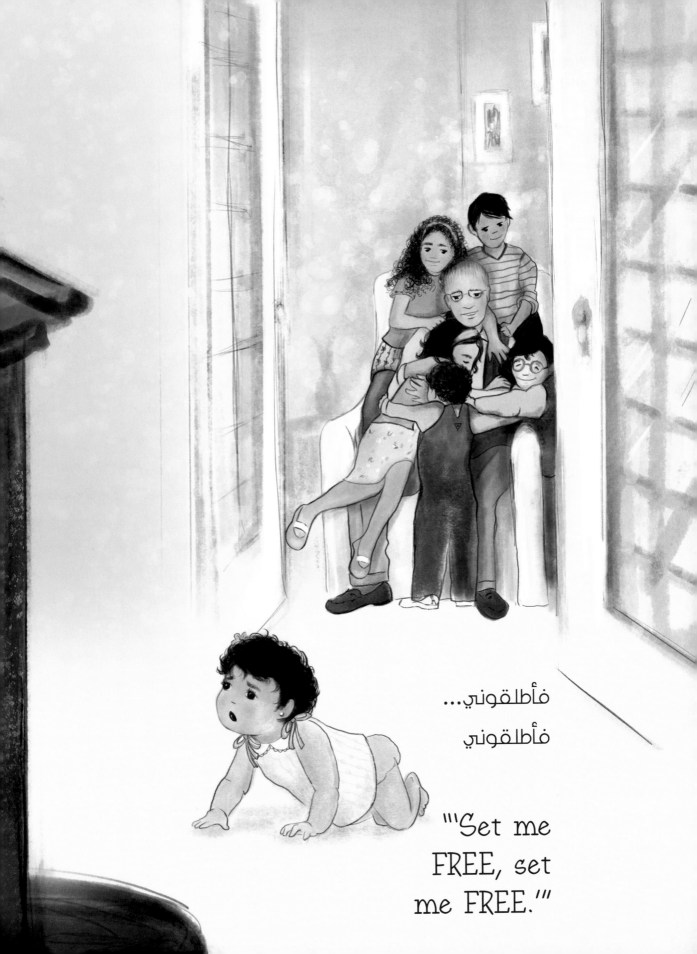

فأطلقوني...
فأطلقوني

"'Set me
FREE, set
me FREE.'"

عن الشاعر

الأنشودة التي غناها بابا سليمان في القصة هي أنشودة كان يغنيها والد الكاتبة لها وهي صغيرة..وهي جزء من قصيدة للشاعر العراقي معروف الرصافي (١٨٧٥- ١٩٤٥م). كان الرصافي شاعراً، معلماً، وأديباً. ويعتبر الرصافي من أهم شعراء العراق في القرن الماضي، نادى بالحرية ومقاومة الاستعمار الأجنبي حتى أنه عُرف بشاعر الحرية.

https://ar.m.wikipedia.org/wiki

ABOUT THE POET

The song BaBa Soliman was singing is part of a poem by the Iraqi poet **Ma'ruf Al Rusafi** (1875–1945). Al Rusafi was a poet, educationist, and a literary scholar. He is considered by many to be a controversial figure in modern Iraqi literature due to his advocacy of freedom and opposition to imperialism and is known as the *poet of freedom*. The author's father used to sing this song to her as a child. She knows he is singing it in the heavens with all of the beautiful, free birds.

Have a book idea?
Contact us at:

info@mascotbooks.com | www.mascotbooks.com